D1194504

Copyright © 2012 by Dale Hayes
First Edition – December 2012

Illustrated by: Diane Lajoie

ISBN
978-1-4602-0428-3 (Paperback)
978-1-4602-0429-0 (eBook)

All rights reserved.

No part of this publication may be reproduced in any form, or by any means, electronic or mechanical, including photocopying, recording, or any information browsing, storage, or retrieval system, without permission in writing from the publisher.

Produced by:

FriesenPress
Suite 300 – 852 Fort Street
Victoria, BC, Canada V8W 1H8

www.friesenpress.com

Distributed to the trade by The Ingram Book Company

KC

Enjoy!
Dale Hayes
2014

Dedicated to the most important people
in my life...my boys.

Thank you for the inspiration.

Hi! I'm KC.. the good little Diggy Dog who does naughty things!

I used to live at a shelter with lots of other Diggy Dogs just like me. I liked the shelter, even though sometimes I had to stay in my cage because I did something naughty. I spent a lot of time in my cage.

At the shelter, I never had any toys of my own to play with...all the Diggy Dogs had to share. Some Diggy Dogs do not like sharing.

I dreamed and dreamed that, some day, I would have a Mommy and Daddy to take me home.

One day, my
Mommy and
Daddy came
to the shelter.
They had
dreams too...
they dreamed of having a
Diggy Dog, just like me, of
their very own. Sometimes,
dreams do come true.

When I first met Mommy and Daddy, I was so excited that I made pee pee on the shelter floor.

I know that making pee pee on the floor
is a naughty thing to do, but Mommy
didn't mind cleaning it up because she
already loved me.

Mommy and Daddy even gave me my very own toys: a teddy bear, a pull toy, and a yellow rubber ducky. I like my rubber ducky the best. They gave me a new red bandana too!

Mommy and Daddy have a big car. On the way home, Daddy opened the window. I put my head out and felt the wind on my face.

Mommy kept telling me to put my head back into the car but I didn't listen. Daddy was laughing but Mommy wasn't. She was worried about me, so Daddy closed the window.

Mommy laid my head in her lap and we cuddled all the way home. I love being cuddled because it makes me feel so happy.

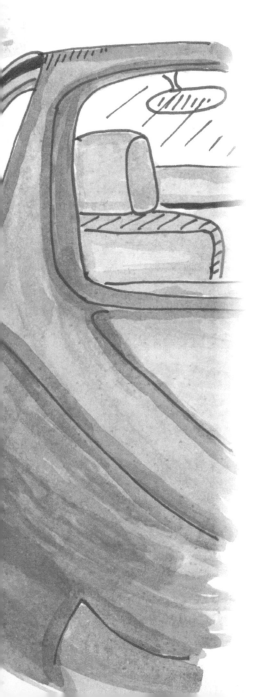

When I saw my new house,
I was so excited! I couldn't
wait to jump out of the car
and start my new adventure
with Mommy and Daddy.

 I'm KC...the good little Diggy Dog who does naughty things. I'm finally home!

CPSIA information can be obtained
at www.ICGtesting.com
Printed in the USA
LVIW02n1932041213
363901LV00001B/2